Family Storybook Library

Let Your Heart
Be Your Guide

Stories About Happiness

∽◦◦◦◦∼

BOOK ELEVEN

BOOK ELEVEN

Let Your Heart Be Your Guide

Stories About Happiness

Introduction

Often, the very thing that fills a situation with joy and humor is its sheer unexpectedness. There are many reasons to be happy. If we're lucky enough to enjoy good health, or a loving family, or good friendships, we're very lucky indeed. But if we can find joy in unexpected ways, we've opened ourselves up to a whole new world of delight. Happiness has a hard time entering a closed heart.

Both Belle and Duchess find happiness in unorthodox ways. Duchess never dreams of finding love and companionship in the form of O'Malley. Belle is happiest with the new adventures that books bring—behavior not normally associated with the girls in her village. Both open their hearts and minds to new adventures and thus cannot keep happiness from them.

The Aristocats' Adventure

from *The Aristocats*

———— ∞∞∞ ————

There are times when you have to be lost before you can find a new road.

Duchess and her kittens, Toulouse, Berlioz, and Marie, were aristocats. That meant that they had very fine manners and lived a comfortable life in an elegant house in Paris. Madame, their owner, loved them very much, and had her butler Edgar make sure that their every need was taken care of. Edgar always did as he was asked, but deep down, he was very jealous of the cats.

One night Edgar overheard Madame telling her lawyer that she was planning on

leaving her entire fortune to her pets. Edgar was furious. He wanted that money for himself! He knew he had to act fast. That night, Edgar kidnapped the aristocats and abandoned them in the country.

"Where are we, Mama?" Marie asked, shivering in the cold.

Duchess looked around. The countryside was very different from the fancy city she was used to. All she could see were trees and grass and a blue sky. She heard birds chirping and a stream bubbling. Then, she heard something else. It was a big alley cat singing!

The cat stopped singing and stared when he saw Duchess. He had never seen such a beautiful cat before. His name was O'Malley, and when he met the kittens, he knew he had to help. Soon the cats were on their way back to the city.

Paris was very far away, but with O'Malley, the trip was an adventure. The cats climbed aboard a milk truck for a ride, then pretended to be a train when they came to some train tracks. And it was very exciting when Marie fell in the river and O'Malley bravely rescued her. By the end of the day, the little ones were very tired from all they had done.

"We'd better stop for the night," O'Malley told Duchess. "I have a pad right over there. It isn't fancy, but it's nice and quiet."

Just then a loud blast from a trumpet burst from the window of O'Malley's pad. His alley-cat friends had come by, and were having a party.

"These cats really know how to swing!"
O'Malley told Duchess.

Duchess loved O'Malley's friends. They

played music and sang and danced until the kittens couldn't keep their eyes open anymore. At last, the party ended.

"I think Mama likes Mr. O'Malley," the kittens whispered sleepily to each other.

Duchess did like O'Malley. He had shown her a life she had never known before. He was not an aristocat, but that didn't bother her. He was smart, brave, funny, and very kind. Duchess

knew that with him by her side, she and
her kittens would have nothing to fear.

Belle's Books

from *Beauty and the Beast*

Sometimes the most exciting place to be is in the middle of a book.

henever Belle came to town, the people there began to whisper among themselves.

"There goes Belle, the inventor's daughter," they said. "She's beautiful, but so . . . different."

Belle was different. Other people were happy to spend their whole lives in the tiny town, seeing the same faces every day, doing the same things from one year to the next. Not Belle. She dreamed of romance, adventure, and a life beyond her little world.

No matter how busy she was, Belle always
stopped at the bookshop whenever she came
to town.

"Good morning!" she called as the doorbell rang merrily.

The bookshop owner smiled. Not many people in town loved books the way Belle did, and he was always glad to see her.

"I have some new books today, Belle," he told her. Her face lit up.

"Adventures?" she asked breathlessly. "Love stories? Fairy tales?"

"All three," the shopkeeper replied, piling her arms with books. Then he winked. "And don't finish them all in one day this time, or you won't have anything to read tomorrow!"

Belle laughed. "That's all right. I'll just read

them all over again!"

The books were heavy as she walked out of the store, but Belle didn't mind. Then Gaston reached for one of them.

Gaston knew nothing about books. All he cared about was himself.

"Why do you waste your time *reading?*" he asked Belle. "You could be spending more time with me."

Belle quickly took her book and got away from him. At last she sat down and opened the biggest book. With Gaston gone and sheep grazing on some flowers nearby, Belle was finally able to begin her story.

"Once upon a time, in a faraway land," she read, "a handsome prince was trapped in a fairy's spell . . ." Belle sighed happily. This was just the kind of book she loved. Sometimes she couldn't wait to see how a story ended, and tried to guess what would happen right from the start.

Belle didn't have much time to wonder about it, though, for at that moment, her father called out for her.

"Oh, Papa!" she sighed, closing her book. "I guess my adventure with a handsome

prince is going to have to wait!" And with
a wave good-bye to the sheep, she headed
for home.